IONE
A Sea Witch's Tale

PREQUEL TO AQUOSVEGNA: THE WATER KINGDOM Trilogy

Mayumi Cruz

For a more enjoyable reading experience, read this AFTER Ione: A Sea Witch's Tale:

**AQUOSVEGNA: THE TRIDENT OF POWER
(Book 1 of Aquosvegna: The Water Kingdom)**

* * *

**OTHER BOOKS
BY MAYUMI CRUZ**
Available on
WWW.MAYUMI-CRUZ.COM
or send Message to
www.facebook.com/MayumiCruzAuthorPage/

Fantasy Suspense - Aquosvegna: The Water Kingdom Trilogy
**AQUOSVEGNA: THE TRIDENT OF POWER
(Book 1)**

Dark Fantasy
THE INQUISITOR: A DYSTOPIAN DARK FANTASY

Mythology Fantasy
THE BLACK WIDOW

Psychological Thriller
2019 Best Published Story by Penmasters League Phils.
CHROMA HEARTS

CHAPTER 1

The hard slap on her face was more painful than the scalding kiss of the molten rock which struck her arm.

Reeling from the force of the blow, Ione wobbled and would have fallen to the ocean floor if not for her echo, Jella. The short but sturdy tentacles of the six-inch gelatinous, transparent octopus braced themselves against her back and slowly stood her upright. "I have you, Ione," her echo's voice drifted to her brain, linked to hers.

But her ordeal was far from over.

"Why do you insist on disobeying me, Ione?" Aquilla yelled, her eyes burning with fury. "Do you not respect me as your mother? I have told you many times not to fiddle with the Crocus, and you still do! Now you have even built this place without my knowledge!"

Her head reeling, Ione touched her hurting face. She was certain she will have a bruise tomorrow. *Again.*

She was no match for her mother's strength, the Grand Dame of the Aquaean Keepers of the Crocus, a rare purple flowering plant which grew on land and perpetually supplied by their counterpart human Keepers to Aquosvegna, the Water Kingdom they belonged to. Ambrosia to all Aquaeans, the

Crocus gave them youth, vitality and strength. It also amplified the innate abilities and magical powers of a few select Aquaeans in the royal line of the Originators. Most of all, it intensified the power of the King's Trident.

"I-I was just trying out a recipe, Mother," she murmured, her head hung low. "Surely, it isn't against the Laws."

"What did you say? A *recipe?*" Her mother practically hurled the word as if it was vomit. "That is a *human* word!"

Mortified at the slip of her tongue, Ione bit her lip. What punishment will her mother bestow upon her if she found out about *the book?* Trying not to panic, her eyes wandered around the scullery, past the broken clay pots, the chunks of red-hot magma, and the scattered purple flowers of the Crocus.

She inwardly breathed a sigh of relief when she saw Jella sitting snugly over the book on the pearl table, its arms and body spread out like an umbrella, completely covering it.

"Do not fret, Ione. She will not find this book," Jella's voice again communicated through telepathy.

She allowed herself a ghost of a smile, grateful for her loyal companion.

Her mother misinterpreted it, though, as yet another blow landed on her other cheek.

"You impertinent child!" Her harsh voice filled the secret, tiny place. "You spoke with Meredith, didn't you? You know we do not speak to humans when we come ashore! We do not mingle with them and make friends. We only take what is rightfully ours, which is the Crocus! I should not have taken you to the human Keepers. From now on, Aimon will take Merleia in the Expeditions. You are to remain here with me as server for the royal household."

CHAPTER 2

ong after her mother had gone, Ione remained crouched on the ocean floor, her arms around knees huddled to her chest. Jella was at her feet, forlorn as her. Around them, fishes swam past, unaware of the storm raging inside her.

Aquilla destroyed everything in the underwater cave she'd found and claimed as her sanctuary: the magma rocks she had meticulously set up in the likeness of a human stove, the clay pots she discovered in a shrunken ship, the glasses and spoons. She took away all the Crocus flowers and leaves, even the corms she'd carefully hidden under the table. Afterward, her mother sealed off the cave with a boulder.

As Aquaeans, they can not only swim underwater. They can also effortlessly breathe, walk and move through water like humans did on land by means of the gills hidden under their jaw, the only thing distinguishing them from the Land Creatures. Yet Ione had always envied the humans for the air they breathe, the skies under their heads, their colorful clothes and vibrant homes.

Today, though, she was thankful she lived under the ocean. It enabled her tears to blend in with the salty water, rendering them invisible. Her blue eyes were like cascading waterfalls as uncontrolled tears outpoured.

"I have been looking all over for you, Ione," a deep, kind voice was heard above her.

She looked up into the coral-colored irises of Jarl. Towering over her at six feet, his handsome, square-shaped face smiled down at her. He offered his hands and she took them as she shakily stood up before curtsying before him. Jarl wasn't the Crown Prince, but he deserved the title Prince and the respect it carried. As the lone first cousin and second in line to the throne, he had been raised in the Castle of Aquosvegna.

"You're crying," Jarl frowned. He grasped her chin and tilted her face to his. "And you have bruises."

Ione closed her eyes painfully. Jarl had always been perceptive of her moods since they were children.

The bruises, though. Her mother must have hit her harder than before—*than ever*—for them to appear quite so suddenly.

"Why did Aquilla do this to you this time?"

He knew the abuse she received from her mother. All of Aquosvegna knew. Yet no one can do anything about it, even the King with all his powers. As her mother, Aquilla owned her, and as such, she can do anything she pleased with her—despite the fact that Ione alone gained the brunt of her bursts of anger. To everyone else, Aquilla was pleasant and even charming at times.

"It doesn't matter," she muttered, opening her eyes but keeping them lowered.

Lately, Jarl's meaningful gazes made her uncomfortable. She didn't want to put anything to it, but she noticed it started twelve weeks ago, when she and the Crown Prince began their affair. His actions confused her. He was the one who brought them together and continued to do so by being an intermediary for their trysts.

The thought brought her back to what Jarl spoke of first. "You said you were looking for me, Prince Jarl?"

Her formal address of him caused a slight tic in his jaw before he smiled warmly. "The Crown Prince wants to see you tonight."

Her mood at once changed, her face shining like a precious stone in utter joy. The Castle had been sealed from the inside for a week now, for reasons unknown to the citizenry. There was a rumor that the King ordered it after his Trident went missing for a night, only to find it under his royal bed. The King must have allowed security to be lax, seeing that the Trident was safe.

Ione was overjoyed at the prospect of being with the Crown Prince. She needed to see Leif. She needed to tell him something of utmost importance.

CHAPTER 3

They were in their own little world, a sunken pirate ship a few hundred kilometers from the Castle. They had just made love under a blanket of swaying kelp in a once grand bed, the ebb of the ocean around them humming a sweet melody.

Ione traced her finger along Leif's cheekbone, puzzled at the sudden sharpness at its edges, when weeks ago there wasn't. The Crown Prince's face was shaped like a heart, giving him kind, soft features with his green hair and clear, emerald-green irises. But tonight, his skin felt flaky and scaly. Her fingers started to gently rub it.

Abruptly, he caught her hand, bringing it to his lips. "I've missed you, my Jewel," speaking his term of endearment for her. "How have you been?"

Her thoughts quickly turned to the more urgent matter to discuss with him.

"I-I have something to tell you, my Prince."

"Ione, I told you, when it's just us, you don't have to call me that. You are my Jewel, and you can call me anything other than Prince." His dark brows curled as he gazed at her worried face. "What is it? You're shaking."

"My Prince. . . my love," she added when she saw him shook his head, then she blurted out before she lost courage, "I am with child." She swallowed. *"Your child."*

The shock on his gorgeous face terrified her. She knew, even before she agreed to this affair, that there was no future for them together. The Laws forbade the union of the Keepers clan with the lineage of Originators where the Crown Prince was descended. It was the one and only union forbidden among Aquaeans.

"My child...," muttering, Leif grabbed a handful of his hair and sat up, his back to her.

She hastened to appease him. "Do not be alarmed, my love. No one will ever know you are the father of this child. I will raise him alone." She knew her family will disown her and send her away, but she was prepared to suffer if it meant her beloved would be spared.

He didn't speak for a few minutes, deep in thought. Then, slowly, he turned to her, his eyes heavily burdened.

"I didn't want to tell you this tonight. But it is unavoidable, considering the circumstances." He exhaled a troubled breath. "The King already knows about us."

Seeing her face lit up with hope, he hastened to add, "Ione, he was so furious at me that he threatened to banish me to Polarus. He wanted me to end our affair. It is the reason he ordered the Castle sealed. But I couldn't bear to be without you. I barely managed to slip away from the guards tonight."

"Oh, my love..."

"And when he learns you are carrying my child, I am certain he will impose the Laws to the letter. That means..."

"I will be executed together with my child," she finished his sentence, her lips trembling with fear.

He gathered her in his arms, and for a few moments, she allowed herself to be lulled by the warmth of his embrace.

"There is no way the King will defy the Laws, my love. This is my fate, and so I accept it without any regret of loving you," she whispered, her shoulders drooping in defeat.

Suddenly, Leif's head lifted. "Ione...there *could* be a way."

"What do you mean?"

"If I am King, I can abolish the Law pertaining to the union between our two clans."

She gasped as she understood what he meant. "You can't possibly think...he's your father, my love!"

"And a hindrance to our future together. As well as the future of Aquosvegna!"

He grasped both her shoulders, his voice rising with emotion.

"The King is a slave to the Laws. He would rather kill a woman with child than change the Laws, though he has the power to do so. And he sits on his throne, merely watching the

Water Kingdom and all its creatures being trampled upon, used up and abused by humans. He turns a blind eye to all the trash dumped by those despicable beings in our territories, to all the fishes and plants dying of pollution, to all the water creatures being captured and eaten mercilessly. If he rules much longer, there wouldn't be anything left of Aquosvegna."

"I...I didn't know you felt this way," she frowned. "I always thought you and the King shared the same principles toward humans as your ancestors before you."

Leif pressed his mouth together, his jaws tightening. "I couldn't let him know. But with me as King, not only can I abolish that ludicrous Law against us, I can also make

Aquosvegna great once again. Aquosvegna will reign not only over water but also over land. We will make the humans fear the very name of Aquosvegna!"

"But..."

He gathered her in his arms as he stroked her blue hair. "I love you, Ione, and I want to share my life with you. I want us to raise our child together. I don't want to lose you both."

Her heart leapt happily at his words. How can it not? He was her one true love, *her only love*. Nevertheless, she hesitated.

"The King has been anything but good to me, my love. And the humans, too. They only need to be reminded and guided on the ways of the Water, not punished."

"My Jewel, your heart is pure and kind. But I believe the humans are not worth the effort. Since the time of my great great grandfather, they have violated the agreement set forth by my ancestors. They need to be put in their place. They will not change. And more so, the King. There is no other way for us to be together!"

"Oh, my darling, don't say that. Maybe if you talk to the King again? About us, and about your sentiments about humans? Maybe he would listen with an understanding heart."

Sadly, Leif shook his head. "Ione. . . he forbade me to tell you this, but he already arranged for me to wed the daughter of Narno of Polarus immediately after the Games."

"Wed?" Ione found it hard to breathe. Leif was marrying someone else, while she and her child were doomed!

She cried, "How can the King be so *unfair?* How can he be so *heartless* as to punish me and our child—*his own grandchild*—for simply falling in love?"

"You see now, my Jewel, how Father lives by the Laws." Leif's voice took on an urgency she hadn't heard before. "But when I am King, with you by my side, we can change the Laws, we can change the humans. *Together.* Let us make this a reality, my Queen."

She gazed upon his eyes and found only love and hope for their future. Her heart soared. Slowly, she nodded. "But...how? When? He is heavily guarded at all times."

For the first time that night, Leif grinned, visibly relieved. Then, he told her urgently, "In four days, the Decennial Games will be held. Your family serves the Crocus to him at the ceremonial dinner before the final fight. It is the only food he eats on that occasion, for it amplifies the power of the Trident, a part of which he bestows as a reward to the victor. Can you put poison in it?"

She frowned, thinking hard. "No, the Crocus will merely expunge it from itself for self-preservation. But I think it *can* be a poison if I throw in other elements without my mother noticing it..."

His eyes widened with glee. "You have been exploring like I told you to? Were you able to get Meredith's book?"

"Yes, my love," she demurely smiled. "I tried a concoction from it today, following the instructions. It made my bruise disappear."

At the mention of her bruise, Leif's face turned stormy. "Yet another reason to act now. I, as King, will see to it that your mother receives the punishment she deserves for the way she treats you."

She threw herself at him, and he caught her in a tight embrace. She couldn't be any happier. The future, at last, seemed bright.

Chapter 4

The blaring sound of the large shell trumpets signalled the beginning of the final fight of the Decennial Games.

The Reunion Games, as it was also called, were held every ten years among the chosen fighters of the Five Guardians and the King's champion. The Five Guardians were stewards of the five main oceans of Aquosvegna: Polarus, Atlantica, Placius, Indius, and Antartica. Four of the five—Narno, Surio, Ullu, and Otrus—were cousins of the King. Jarl's father, Jaron of Atlantica, was the King's only brother. All of them descended from the line of the Originators.

Deafening din filled the magnificent underwater arena. Multi-stepped rock formations where the Aquaean audience was seated surrounded an oval clearing of white, powder-textured sand floor. Big and small marine creatures of various kinds, colors, and temperament hovered above—echos of Aquaeans below—serving both as a dome for the structure and as a camouflage, lest humans unwittingly came upon them.

On an elevated area at the northernmost part, the King sat on his throne holding the Trident, while his brother and the four stewards were placed on opposite sides of the platform. He had just finished dining on steamed purple Crocus flowers. Aquilla stood beside Ione behind the throne, while her husband Oric, and their other children, Aimon and Merleia—stood behind the stewards, prepared to heed the King's command to clear the royal oyster plates.

As the two final fighters—Leif and Jarl—marched to the center of the arena, the King gripped the Trident's staff with his right hand. His hand glowed brightly at once, as did the Trident. Ione realized he was transferring the power of the Crocus to it. With his left hand, the King signalled for the duel to begin.

The two princes' silver weapons clashed—Leif's sword and Jarl's saber—as they fought amidst the loud howls and shouts from the crowd.

From the start, Ione sensed something wasn't right. While Leif was his usual easy-going self, treating the game as it was—an occasion for their blood kin to come together in the spirit of camaraderie and fight for a chance to be granted additional power by the Trident—Jarl seemed to be driven by a strange kind of rage. He was continuously on the offense, jabbing at his cousin with more force than she had seen before in their sparrings.

As the fight went on, Leif's smile slowly fell off as he struggled to counter each one of Jarl's attacks, which became fiercer and fiercer. Even the crowd's shouts diminished as the two equally skilled warriors battled it out with every heavy stroke of their weapon.

In one heart-stopping instance, Ione gasped as Jarl's saber almost sliced through Leif's neck. *What was Jarl doing?* It was as if he was not fighting after the power of the Trident, but after something else.

A niggling thought persisted in her mind. *What if Leif told Jarl about their child?* Her heart thumped in her chest.

If he did, it would explain Jarl's violent actions in the arena. His jealousy of Leif, which she'd sensed he harbored since they were young, must have intensified upon learning about her condition. Jarl always had that cruel streak in him.

Her head swelled. Yes, Jarl was fighting after something else today. He was fighting to kill Leif.

It was a fight to the death.

Suddenly, her attention was diverted to the Trident. The glow was decreasing, which meant that the transfer of power from the Crocus was nearing completion. It was the sign she was wating for.

When moments ago, she had been reluctant to go through with it, now she knew she had to.

For Leif.

The commotion that would ensue out of her action will break the fight, and his life would be saved from his vicious cousin's relentless attacks. She had to do this *now*.

Dragging her anxious eyes away from her lover, her lips began to whisper the chant.

Teeth of shark, eye of whale,

tail of snake, heed my wail;

Turn the Crocus to a venom,

bite the King with thy poison.

But her mother heard her low murmur. With unbelieving eyes and mouth agape, Aquilla turned to her. Comprehension dawned on her face as she realized what she was doing.

Quickly, Aquilla put her hand over her mouth and hissed, "Stop it! Stop chanting! *Stop the curse!*"

But Ione couldn't hear her. The energy that was filling her entire body was so incredibly powerful that it drowned her mother's voice and all the noise and beings around her. Her eyes could only see the object of her chant: the King, who was now writhing in terrible pain, causing the Trident to fall to his feet.

As she continued to whisper against her mother's lips, euphoria surged through Ione. A dynamic force, invisible to others but herself, poured out of her body and charged at the King. He collapsed to the platform floor with a loud thud, his whole body shuddering violently. His echo, a great blue whale, let out a loud roar before dropping to the center of the arena from above, barcly missing the two fighters.

The crowd screamed. Chaos ensued. The stewards stood up, knocking back their seats and yelling for the royal guards. Aquilla dashed to the King's side, after roughly pushing Ione—weak and depleted of strength—toward Oric and Aimon, who at once seized her in a vise-like grip.

The fighting stopped, with Leif bolting through the water to attend to his father, Jarl a few feet behind him. In seconds, the Crown Prince arrived at his father's side.

But he was too late. The King was eerily still. He was no longer breathing.

Ione weakly smiled. She had succeeded. *She had saved Leif's life.*

Then, something else happened. It started with the King's fingernails. They turned black. But the blackness didn't stop there. It crawled fast, upward, to his hands and arms, to his neck and face, and his entire body—until he was consumed by it. His once golden, patrician features were gone, replaced by stark ebony.

"Father!" Leif shouted, his green eyes confused. "What is this? What kind of illness is this?"

Across him, Aquilla replied in a shaky voice, "H-he has been poisoned, my Prince."

"Poisoned?" Leif's face grew thunderous. "The King cannot be killed by anything or anyone! The Trident protects him!"

Upon mention of the Trident, all eyes searched for it and found it laid down at the King's feet. There was an audible gasp as everyone in the platform watched the blackness also starting to crawl up its staff.

And then, there was Jarl's saber, almost touching the Trident—which was beginning to turn black, too. He shoved it away, causing his hand to hover above the Trident. For a second, he paused, before he picked up the Trident and stood up, his coral-colored irises focused on Leif.

Before he can take a step though, his body twitched, racked by a great tremor. He dropped the Trident and bent over, shouting in extreme pain.

By all indications, he was also poisoned at the mere touch of the King's weapon. Everyone scampered away from the Trident.

Suddenly, Aquilla's shrill, penetrating voice rose above the gasps and yells.

Oh, powerful Crocus, I call on thee;

defeat thy black enemy!

Strike it down, let it be gone,

wash the venom out of thee!

Ione stared at her mother. She had never heard her chant. Her voice was firm, her words were clear, as if she had done it many times before.

In just three chants, a change occurred. The water around Jarl and the Trident rose and spun around until a large spout formed. It encircled them, rotating wildly. Round and round, faster and faster it went, like a spinning wheel out of control, until finally, it exploded into different directions.

When Ione's vision cleared, the Trident had returned to its original color of gold, its brightness blinding. Jarl was unconscious, but breathing.

Her mother had saved him from certain death and reversed the spell on the Trident.

Her chant overpowered Ione's. It meant she had knowledge about what the humans knew, and she *practiced* it.

She wasn't given a chance to ask Aquilla, for her father and siblings dragged her away forcefully in that instant.

As they exited the platform, she looked over her shoulder to see Leif talking to her mother. His eyes caught hers.

She drew in her breath sharply, her heart suddenly anxious.

For instead of love and triumph, she saw in them disbelief and contempt.

CHAPTER 5

When the newly-crowned King entered the prison where Ione had been incarcerated for two days, her relief was visible. But it quickly vanished when she saw her mother, along with all the stewards, were with him.

A feeling of dread descended upon her. Leif didn't come to take her away from there and make her Queen as she had hoped. He came for another thing entirely.

Jaron of Atlantica spoke the words of doom.

"Ione of the Keepers clan, you have been found guilty of murdering King Prius of Aquosvegna, inflicting harm on Prince Jarl, and involving yourself in human affairs. You and your echo are sentenced to death three hours from now before the general assembly. King Leif thus so decrees."

"No. *No!*" Ione screamed as Jella clung to her arm. She gripped the thick coral bars and cried, "My love, why are you doing this? You said. . ."

The new King squinted at her, furious at what she uttered. "What did you call me? Ione, I may have known you since we were children, but I have only always treated you as *a friend.* And my Father treated you kindly. That is why I absolutely loathe what you did!"

"A friend?" She almost laughed. "How can you say that, when we have been intimate and are going to have a child together?"

"Are you insane?" Leif's face turned volatile. His wrath was so palpable, she took a step back as though he had struck her with the very Trident he was holding. He bared his teeth, his voice booming like thunder, hurting her ears and crushing her heart.

"I wouldn't allow myself to touch you intimately, much more beget a child with you! You are a despicable, evil murderess! Say no more of your lies, Ione, or else you will not only be put to death, your name shall never be spoken of in Aquosvegna ever again!"

Then he turned his back on her and marched out.

And at that exact moment, Ione ceased to live.

CHAPTER 6

I know you have the book, Ione. Give it to me." Her mother waited until the last of the royal guards had walked out of the prison before speaking to her.

She heard her, but her entire body was numb. Her back was slumped against the coral bars, head hung low and hands down to her sides.

Jella's squeal woke her up from her stupor. She felt her echo's fright before its voice penetrated her brain: "Ione, *help!*"

She stood up and found her mother squeezing Jella's small, fragile body. She had snatched the poor creature from beyond the bars.

"Give me the book, Ione, or I will strangle her dead," she snarled.

Ione's eyes flared as she remembered, "You knew about the book all along. You knew how to use it, Mother. Why? How?"

"The book, Ione. Give it to me and I will tell you." Briefly, Aquilla's face softened. "I'll grant you that before the Trident strikes you down today."

Exhaling, Ione reached down and pulled up the full, flowing seaweed skirt of her dress. The book was tied tightly around her inner hip by several threads of her long, blue hair. Once untied, she handed it over to Aquilla, who reverently took it with shaking hands, releasing Jella.

"I thought I would never see this again," she whispered. "You stole this from Meredith, didn't you?"

"Yes," Ione replied, beyond caring, "if you want to call it that. It wasn't even kept under lock and key. Meredith called it a recipe book." She remembered opening the book, awed at finding potions, curses, and spells, while Meredith only ever saw food recipes.

Her mother nodded. "It is because the book is enchanted." A sinister smile graced her lips. "Getting this book is the only act of good for which I will remember you by."

"But you still haven't answered me, Mother. How come you knew about this book?"

Aquilla hissed, "Because this is *my* book. This belongs to my ancestors!"

Shocked, Ione took a step back. "Y-yours? I don't understand. How did it come upon Meredith's hands? She's a human Keeper!"

"Her father tricked me into giving this to him after he befriended me, and then seduced me."

Ione's confusion escalated. "But a human and an Aquaean cannot have any kind of relations. You should have been sentenced to death, too."

Her mother's silence was deafening. She drew a sharp breath. "The King *knew*. He knew and he concealed it. Why?"

Her mother lifted her chin. "The line of Keepers cannot be broken or passed on to anyone else. He had to compromise."

"And Meredith's father?"

"He received his just punishment. But before we can reclaim the book, he put a powerful spell to it—a spell he learned from me. No Aquaean can take it from his home."

Ione's brows furrowed. "I don't understand. I was able to get it effortlessly."

"No Aquaean," Aquilla gave her a sharp look. ". . . except for his *own blood*."

"His own. . . ," Ione's head swirled. "Mother, you can't mean. . ."

"Yes," Aquilla jeered. "The King's punishment unto me was to make me keep and raise you here in Aquosvegna. Perhaps he hoped you would get the book back for me someday. Alas, he didn't foresee *you* killing him with it."

Ione's head was spinning fast. She gripped the coral bars to make herself stable. "And *you. . . ,*" she gritted her teeth, *"you punished me* by hating me all my life."

Her mother was uncontrite. "You were the offspring of a lowly human who deceived me into possessing the most powerful book in the world. What did you expect?"

When before she was consumed by numbness, now Ione felt a hot, burning rage building up inside her. The *injustice* of it all—

her mother's forbidden affair and subsequent impunity, the King's prejudice, her father's death, her ordeal since childhood under her mother's cruelty, and presently, for being used and rejected by Leif to usurp the throne of Aquosvegna.

Like deep ocean currents, her rage upwelled to the surface, spilling out of her lips.

Why me? Why me?

When everything was her fault?

Grant me justice, justice,

for suffering it all.

It became a low chant but with a powerful intensity which her mother didn't notice until it was too late.

A single strand of Ione's hair still tied around the book loosened, sprung forth, and entered her mother's nose. It quickly went down to her heart, trussed it, and sliced it into pieces. She fell down, dead, not knowing what struck her.

The coral bars crumpled like dust under Ione's hands, freeing her from her cage. Jella quickly took the book and brought it to her. As she held it in her hands, her waist-long, blue hair lifted, swirled, and embedded itself into the pages of the book like a woven tapestry. Then, as if a razor had cut through it, it detached itself from her, leaving her with enough hair which quickly grew back to its original length.

Her father's spell was more powerful than Aquilla had thought. It not only enabled her to get the book. *It also attached the book to her, making her its master.*

She smiled bitterly. Her father wasn't just a lowly human, after all. He had magical powers, the extent of which her mother never knew about.

And those powers were passed on to her. *. . his daughter.* Powers which filled her with unbelievable energy. Powers she can use to exact revenge.

Her nostrils flared as her mind went back to the indignity she suffered. Leif will pay for his degradation of her. Not only him, and not only for a finite time. She wanted him to suffer for all time.

As if hearing her thoughts, hair strands came out of the book, flipped the pages, and settled on a particular one.

Eternal Curse

Yes! Her mood soared. Feverishly, she scanned the ingredients. There were only four required to cast the curse.

One Crocus corm

A fragment of black heart

A piece of your soul

And the tie that binds

She muttered, "Where will I get these things? I don't have access to the Crocus anymore. And I don't understand what the other three are."

Jella swam to her, opened its mouth, and produced a corm. "I was able to hide one before your mother took everything from the underwater cave," its voice echoed in her mind.

Happily, Ione took it. "But what about the black heart? Where can I find it?"

For answer, a hair strand lifted from the book, pointing it to the lifeless body of Aquilla. "Truly, she had a black heart," she agreed. "But still, she was my mother. I can't cut her open and get a piece of her heart!"

"She's dead, Ione," Jella cooed in her mind. "And she'll only be getting what she deserved for her treatment of you all these years."

She exhaled, bitter memories coming back to her like raging waters. "You're right."

The words had barely left her lips when her hair lifted, dragging her beside her mother's body. Once there, it twirled around her right wrist, pulled it and raised it over Aquilla's chest, which instantly cracked open. A sliver of black flew itself into Ione's palm.

She gagged, but was able to hold back the bile coming up her throat. She put it beside the Crocus corm.

"A piece of my soul," she read the book again. "How can I get that?"

A severed tentacle dropped beside the book. She gasped as she realized Jella had cut if off from itself. "Jella! What did you do?"

"Ione, I am your echo. Your life is linked to me, as I am to yours. I am alive because you are. When you die, I will die, too. Therefore, I am your soul," Jella gently explained to her.

Her eyes tearing up, Ione murmured her gratitude. "You have always been there for me. And now, you've sacrificed a piece of you for me."

"My sacrifice is nothing compared to yours, Ione."

"What do you mean?"

With a somber expression, Jella pointed at the fourth and last ingredient.

"The tie that binds," Ione repeated. "Where do I get this?"

Her hair lifted again, this time, surrounding her waist. At first, she was bewildered, wondering what the book was telling her. Then she felt like the entire water world descended upon her all at once as discernment set in.

Their child—hers and Leif's—was the tie that bound them together. She had to sacrifice her unborn child—and therefore unbind herself from her connection to Leif—to complete the curse.

She touched her stomach with trembling hands. She sobbed as her tears flowed abundantly. Her heart screamed with love for the innocent life growing inside her womb.

Why? Why did she have to sacrifice it? It was blameless, an unassuming victim.

"My child. . . *my blood.*"

But it wasn't just her blood. She blinked as the ugly truth fought with her emotions. Leif's blood was mixed with it.

Leif, who didn't even acknowledge nor care about it. Leif who used her, made her kill, then deceived her, scorned her before the stewards, and had given her to death.

No. Her mind disregarded the frantic pleas of her heart. She will not die. She will get her revenge.

Whatever it took.

CHAPTER 7

In stark contrast to the deafening noise of the Decennial Games, the arena was silent and gloomy at the time of the execution, even as it overflowed with the citizenry and their echos as well as the representatives of the Five Guardians.

They all watched with varied emotions as Ione and Jella were led to the front of the platform. There, a stone-faced Leif and his entourage were gathered.

Ione held her head high and scanned them dispassionately. Leif, green eyes flashing with fury and authority, sat on his precious throne holding the Trident that would bring her death. Her father, brother and sister, as always, stood behind the throne, their faces bearing no traces of concern for her. There were also the five stewards, along with their advisers. Familiar faces of childhood friends stared stoically back at her: Einar, made Head of the guards; and Xyril, as Chief Officer and Adviser—who, with the King, now formed Aquosvegna's Triumvirate.

And then there was Jarl. He looked weak still, after what he had gone through. His head was lowered and his shoulders drooped, as if her impending death pained him. When he met her eyes, she noticed they had changed to a deeper color than before, a probable reaction of his body to the poison. It matched his hair. Red-orange irises which blazed with pity and passion locked with her blue hues, and for an instant, she found solace there, touching her heart like a warm, healing balm.

But her heart was now cold, hardened, and beyond healing.

Jaron, Guardian of Atlantica, stood up. "Ione, you have been sentenced to death for your crimes. You have dishonored the Keepers clan. You are a disgrace to your family, that even your mother is not here, most probably too ashamed to witness your execution. Do you have anything to say?"

"I do." She replied, her voice firm.

"Speak."

Pointing an accusing finger at the King, she did, her voice increasing in volume with every word.

"I curse you, King Leif, and yours after you!

Black for black, soul for soul

Tie unbound, from womb undone

By the power of the Crocus,

these words shall come true!

For all my pain, your life be hell

Never here shall a Queen dwell.

And for every tear you made me shed

Shall be returned to you ten-fold.

For thy heirs shall be the catalyst

For Aquosvegna to cease to exist!

Lest land and water reconcile

Both worlds shall be laid waste and defiled.

Upon you, this is my revenge

So be it, and so shall it be,

Until the world ends.

Aimon shouted, "She's cursing the King! She must be stopped!"

Einar yelled, "Guards, stop her! Restrain her!"

Royal guards surrounded her, but one sweep of her hand and their swords flew, striking them instead. There was an uproar as the crowd shrieked in horror.

Merleia whispered frantically to Xyril, who hurriedly urged Leif, "My King, act now before she repeats the curse to fruition!"

In a flash, Leif threw the Trident at Ione. It pierced her chest, its prongs going through her back. Generous blood spurted. She staggered but remained standing. Still, she chanted repeatedly, loud and strong, her voice making everyone's ears hurt.

"No!" Jarl jumped off the platform, running fast toward her, his arms outstretched. But he couldn't touch her. She had put up an invisible shield around her, a strong magic only the Trident had infiltrated.

He begged, "Ione, stop! You can still live. I shall help you. Let me pull out the Trident and you shall be enlightened about everything. Please, Ione. Please!" He banged on the shield to break it, but it was no use.

But Ione was past enlightenment. Her words drifted to Leif, circling him like sharks hungry for meat. Unseen by all, they penetrated his body and pierced his echo, Magni, a whale shark.

As Ione took her last breath, the curse took effect.

Lifeless, her body briefly became a pillar of salt before dissipating, blending with the saline water of the ocean. The Trident promptly returned to the King's open hand.

It was over. There was a collective sigh of relief from the crowd, who had once again settled down.

No one took notice of Jella drifting away with the grains of sand that was Ione.

CHAPTER 8

Einar placed a sympathetic hand on Jarl's shoulder. The arena was empty. Even so, the new Crown Prince remained kneeling at the very spot where Ione had fallen.

"We grieve as well, my friend. Leif didn't want this any more than you, but it had to be done."

Jarl gritted his teeth. "He could have spared her life. And her child."

"You believed her? All her words were lies. You and I know she wanted Leif ever since we were young. If Leif had indeed succumbed to her seduction, she should have known what she was getting into. A Keeper can never be Queen."

Jarl clenched his fists at his sides. "For you all, she was nothing. She was just another Aquaean girl blinded by awe and adoration for the golden Crown Prince who is now King!"

"Aren't they all?" Einar scoffed. He sighed, "We have to be by your cousin's side. Come, there is much to do for Aquosvegna, my friend. You have an important task at the Castle."

Jarl shook her head. "I am going back to Atlantica. I have already spoken to my Father. I will settle in Bermuda."

"What? Why? The King needs you here."

"If he really needed me here," Jarl growled, "he should have made me his Chief Officer and Adviser, not Xyril."

"You and I know the Laws state that the next in line cannot hold a task of that importance."

"And what task am I worthy of? A decoration by the King's side?"

"You are as important as the King. By being by his side, you will learn everything needed for when you would come to the throne."

"You and I know, my friend," Jarl sneered, "no next in line kin ever comes to the throne. Especially when the King begets a son."

Einar stared at his friend's stiff back. Jarl had always been envious of his cousin's position in the hierarchy of Originators. Nevertheless, he couldn't agree with Leif's suspicion that Jarl intended to kill him during the fight and when he had picked up the Trident at his father's dead feet. What Einar could not understand was why Jarl seemed so affected by the death of Ione, who, if not for Leif, had avoided him at all costs because he scared her.

He had no time for these matters, though. There was much to be done.

"It seems you have made up your mind. I shall tell the King of your decision. I will leave you now, my friend." Einar didn't wait for a reply and immediately turned on his heels.

Alone at last, Jarl scooped a mound of sand with his palm. His echo, Nius the stingray, hovered above, its pectoral fins flapping in rhythm with its owner's beating, broken heart.

A single tear dropped from Jarl's eyes, wetting the sand he was holding as he whispered an elegy for Ione.

"For them, she was nothing of value. But for me, she was a jewel of the sea."

He stood up, letting the grains of sand drift off with the salty waters.

"My sea. My jewel."

With heavy steps, he walked away to prepare for his departure for Bermuda.

72

CHAPTER 9

Far, far away from Aquosvegna, a tiny octopus floated freely in the water. No more than six inches, its semi-translucent body changed colors as it blended with the water current and the marine creatures it passed by. Its prominent ear-like fins flapped gently, navigating its journey, helped along by its seven webbed tentacles.

Underneath one severed tentacle, fastened snugly in its inner membrane, a violet stone rested.

As Jella wiggled all the way up, nearer to the shore, the stone sparkled brightly, vibrantly, like a jewel of the sea.

EPILOGUE:
THE SINS OF THE FATHERS

THREE YEARS LATER

SOUTH CENTRAL SAHARA
DESERT: THE TENERE

T he vast plain of sand stretching from northeastern Niger into the western part of the Republic of Chad was covered in eerie darkness. Above it, the blackness of the skies was peppered by a sprinkling of stars which, although plenty, did not quite give enough illumination over the land.

A newborn's wail pierced through the silence of the desert night, followed by an odd mix of varying tones of whimpers floating amidst the warm, arid wind.

After checking on the source of the wail, and finding it to his satisfaction, the green-haired warrior hurriedly focused his full attention to the woman lying on the sand.

She was on her back, her helmet and warrior suit set aside. Only a white, blood-stained garment covered her battered body.

Her long, white hair fanned her beautiful face, making her features aglow for the last time . . . *for she was dying.*

The man clasped her hands, as he urgently pleaded to her,

"My love, let me find an oasis. There must be one here. . . somewhere. . . !"

"No. . ." the woman whispered, struggling to speak.

"You and I . . . know. . . I am . . . beyond that. There. . . is no time. . . to waste. Do . . . what we have. . . agreed upon. Please, my love. Do not . . . let . . . my death . . . be in vain."

A sob escaped from the man's lips. "Must the cost be this high?"

Weakly, she lovingly touched his face. "I'm afraid. . . it is, my darling. Because . . . what is at stake. . . is comparable . . . to none."

Miserably, he can only stare at her helplessly for he knew what she said was true.

"I can't do this alone. . . I can't do this without you!"

"You will. . . you *must!*"

Eagerly, she squeezed his hand with all the strength remaining in her. His green eyes searched her blue ones, etching her face in his memory.

"I love you. *I love you!*" he murmured pressingly, realizing that they only have seconds to spare.

"And I, you. Always. . . Please. . . remember. . . that."

"I will. I will never forget you, my darling."

One last kiss.

One last breath.

Then she closed her eyes, her hands dropping from his grasp, her breathing expunged.

Slowly, her skin started to shrivel and dry up.

He watched her as her body gradually turned brown and wrinkled, until it took the form of a driftwood, her face and body etched on it. Unmoving, cold, and lifeless.

For a few seconds, the man sat immobile. His grief was indescribable, his agony deeply entrenched in his heart that it rendered him numb. A lone tear escaped from his blank eyes, a last monument to his emotions, before he put it away, never to surface for eternity.

He begun to claw at the sand with his bare hands. At snail's pace at first, but then, it became faster. . . and faster. . . until a shallow grave was formed.

There, he gently laid down the wooden image of the only woman he has ever loved, placing a kiss on its cold lips. Then he covered the grave with the sand he had dug, burying her along with the love in his heart.

Afterward, with shaking hands, he scooped the whimpering newborn in his arms. He slowly put his left palm over the little one's face.

The child cried and cried and cried.

Then the cries abruptly stopped.

His jaw clenched, the green-haired man stood up and walked, with heavy footsteps, back to the direction of the makeshift tent in the middle of the Sahara desert.

Several gruesome tasks were waiting, still to be undertaken. His wife was right. There was no time to waste.

*　*　*

Somewhere in the North Atlantic Ocean, a baby bottle-nosed dolphin, swimming beside its floating dead mother, shrieked a high-pitched, lengthy, depressing whistle.

Then it slowly came beside its mother and rested its head on her exposed stomach. It stayed there, like its mother, unmoving.

EPILOGUE:
A KING'S SACRIFICE

WESTERN PACIFIC OCEAN:

MARIANA TRENCH

Located somewhere in the western Pacific east of the Philippines and east of the Mariana Islands, the Mariana Trench was a crescent-shaped scar in the Earth's crust that measures more than 2,550 kilometers long and 69 kilometers wide.

It was recognized by humans as the deepest part of the world's ocean as well as Earth's deepest location. Geologists claimed that if Mount Everest were dropped into the deepest point of the Mariana Trench, or the Challenger Deep, its peak would still be more than 1.6 kilometers underwater. The Challenger Deep was measured at more than 11,000 meters.

The known depth.

From above, the dark blue waters of the ocean danced in slow rhythm with the gentle wind, the scorching hot sun's rays bouncing on the surface.

Yet 16,000 meters underneath it--an additional five thousand meters deeper than the depth known to man—a storm was brewing.

Hidden from human eyes since time immemorial by gigantic stone formations and nestled in the farthest, deepest nook of this part of the underwater world, a colossal castle sat amid seaweeds and corals.

The castle was cloaked above by gigantic, overlapping shells where glittering, flickering diamonds were embedded, serving doubly as the citadel's source of light.

Its walls were made of sturdy white coral reefs, adorned with chunks of shining, sparkling multi-colored jewels. Its tall towers, twelve in all, stood proudly, guarded by giant yellow sea horses, their heights no less than ten feet tall, with each of their eyes moving independently, following the activity of passing sea life without giving their presence away.

The main gate, situated on the grounds at the middle of the fortress, was comprised of two humongous rocks, each of which is six meters thick. They were manned by two enormous octopuses, hiding in plain sight. For they were almost unnoticeable, their skin's cells and arms' muscles matching the color and texture of the rocks, serving as the first line of defense against attackers.

The entrance gave way to a huge courtyard where a hundred palace guards, dressed in full battle gear, were placed in strategic positions, their booted feet firmly settled on the sandy, white ground. They looked very much like humans, if not for the gills on either side of their jaws, just below the ears, which flap silently as they breathe in through the waters.

The inside of the castle bespoke of incomparable wealth and tasteful sophistication. The floors were made up of slabs of glimmering mother-of-pearls. Thick, deep green seaweed curtains, from which colored jewels hung playfully, cover the walls. Colorful fishes and small marine life freely roam around. Tables, chairs, benches and other furnitures were made up of the finest, smoothest white marble. The stairs leading to the upper floors stood in stark contrast, though, as they were assembled from slabs of elegant black marble.

In the middle of the spacious foyer, a wide stairway led straight to the uppermost floor. It was where the king's private suites are located.

Heavy, echoing footsteps entered the majestic room, treading slowly as the news-bearer traversed the shiny, white pearlized floor.

The messenger stopped, standing before the man sitting on the edge of the enormous four poster bed made up of huge, sturdy planks of multicolored coral reefs, surrounded by a soft, lush cushion of white and green seaweeds.

The man was bowed down, his hands cradling his crown of green hair adorned with scattered flecks of blue and silver.

He lifted his head slightly and asked with a barely audible voice without looking at the newcomer,

"Is it . . . done?"

An uneasy silence ensued for but a few seconds.

The dreaded reply came.

"It is. . . as you commanded."

The man on the bed closed his eyes painfully, gravely nodding.

Then, he remembered to ask, "What. . . what was it?"

An exhale of sorrowful breath was heard, before he was answered,

"They. . . it was a they. They were. . . twins. A boy. . . and a girl."

Upon hearing this, the crouched man wept silently, tearlessly, his shaking shoulders the only indication of the intensity of his emotions.

The newsbearer clenched his jaws and waited in silence for the man to compose himself.

He should know. He had done exactly the same a few days ago.

After some time, the grieving man stood up, his back tensed like a rod. Trying hard to steady his voice, he whispered:

"Then there is one more matter left to do."

The newcomer scowled.

"Forgive me, but I think it unnecessary, especially now. The deed is done. No one knows, except myself."

"You are wrong there. *I know*. And that is something I cannot live with."

"My friend. . ."

The sorrowful man did not wait for him to continue. He earnestly implored him, "I realize this last matter I command you to do is a burden so extreme that I myself know it is unjust and unfair to you. But for the sake of the two worlds, I ask . . . no, *I beg of you*. . . please do this. The prince of Bermuda must never wield the power of the Trident!"

Nodding slowly in agreement, the news-bearer said humbly, "I understand."

The man asked then, his eyes searching: "Where is Merleia? Why is she not with you? Is she outside?"

It was the newsbearer's turn to show grief. "She. . . she did not make it. The journey proved to be. . . too taxing. . . for her condition."

The man gasped out loud. "No! Not her! Why her? This is all my fault! THIS IS ALL MY FAULT!"

Hurriedly, the other man appeased him. "Do not burden yourself, my friend. She knew what she was getting into."

"What about. . ." the man asked.

The look he gave him confirmed his worst fears.

"My friend, I am so, deeply, truly sorry. Please forgive me."

The man slumped back on the bed, weeping profusely.

His friend hastened to pacify him, not wanting to add to the weight of guilt that has tormented him. "There is nothing to forgive. Things happened as they did. This isn't your fault."

"Oh but it is, my friend. If I hadn't. . ."

The news-bearer cut him off earnestly, not wanting him to wallow in useless guilt. He firmly held the other man's shoulders, looking him in the eye.

Dark, deep moss eyes took hold of bright, sparkling, emerald eyes, holding them prisoners to his stare. They looked almost alike, if not for the tinge of their eyes.

"Enough! Let us gaze toward the horizon, beyond our pain, and be thankful that the curse of the Sea Witch will never be fulfilled now. Weep no more, my friend, and let us act swiftly and accordingly. For Aquosvegna!"

Only then did the grieving man saw in his friend's eyes an incomprehensible pain, much like his own. And in there, he also found strength and conviction, borne of the same kind of pain which fuelled his body to action.

He stood up, wiping his tears with the back of his hand. Clasping his friend's shoulders in return, he firmly responded,

"We are kindred souls, you and I. . . in everything. But you are right. I apologize profusely. There are things to do, and emotions have to be extinguished for matters that are far more important."

His friend nodded, his face an image of resolute determination as well, as he replied tonelessly,

"The pain will go away, my friend. And then there would be nothing else but numbness."

"Yes. . .," the other man agreed, and then, bowing his head as he knelt before the news-bearer, ". . . my King. As always, you are right."

Immediately, the other man corrected him,

"No, my King, my Lord," as he, too, knelt in front of his friend, his head bowed lower, his respect and reverence evident toward the man before him.

Continuing, he gravely stated, "It is Aquosvegna who is forever indebted to you.

This is my vow unto you: your sacrifice will not be put to waste."

Then he slowly unleashed the knife strapped to his right leg, its malevolent sound cutting through the stillness of the gloomy, majestic room.

The other man closed his sea-green, emerald eyes and waited for the sharp blade to strike.

* * * THE STORY OF IONE &

AQUOSVEGNA CONTINUES IN

AQUOSVEGNA:

THE TRIDENT OF POWER

(Book 1 of

THE AQUOSVEGNA

TRILOGY)

WHICH CAN ALSO BE PURCHASED
DIRECT FROM THE AUTHOR.
TO PURCHASE, SEND MESSAGE TO

Facebook:www.facebook.com/MayumiCruzAuthorPage/

ABOUT MAYUMI CRUZ

Mayumi Cruz is an award-winning indie author writing diverse, cross-genre fiction. To date, she has published thirteen books and co-authored four anthologies.

Chroma Hearts, her Psychological Thriller novel, was awarded 2019 Best Published Story of the Year by Penmasters' League Philippines, where she was also recognized as 3rd Best Published Author. Some of her writings have also appeared in Philippines Graphic and other online and print publications.

Also an artist, Mayumi holds degrees in Economics and Educational Management.

Her books are available on Amazon and other digital bookstores.

Also available on her:

Website: www.mayumi-cruz.com

Facebook:www.facebook.com/MayumiCruzAuthorPage/